# التيوسِ الثلاثة الاخوة
# The Three Billy Goats Gruff

retold by
Henriette Barkow

illustrated by
Richard Johnson

Arabic translation by Ayser Aljawad

في يومٍ من الأيام كانَ هناكَ ثلاثةُ تيوسٍ جائعونَ يُعرَفونَ بِ "الأخوة جروفْ". كانوا يَعيشونَ على جانبِ تَلٍ شَديدِ الانحدارِ. أَكلَتَ التيوس جروفْ العُشبَ شديدِ الخضرةِ جميعَهُ. والآن هُم في حاجةٍ لِلبَحثِ عنْ طعامٍ.

Once there were three very hungry billy goats called Gruff. They lived on the side of a steep, steep hill. The Billy Goats Gruff had eaten all the green, green grass and needed to find some food.

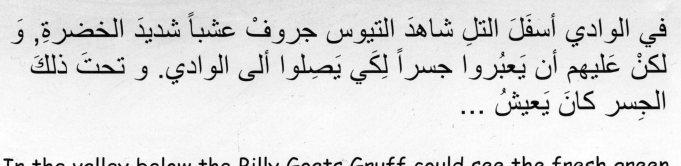

في الوادي أسفَلَ التلِ شاهدَ التيوس جروفْ عشباً شديدَ الخضرةِ, وَ لكنْ عَليهم أن يَعبُروا جسراً لِكَي يَصِلوا ألى الوادي. و تحتَ ذلكَ الجِسر كانَ يَعيشُ ...

In the valley below the Billy Goats Gruff could see the fresh green grass, but to reach it they had to cross over a bridge.
And under that bridge lived a mean and hungry ...

مْئيم ُلئ ع ُجاِئ ع ُدرام.

TROLL!

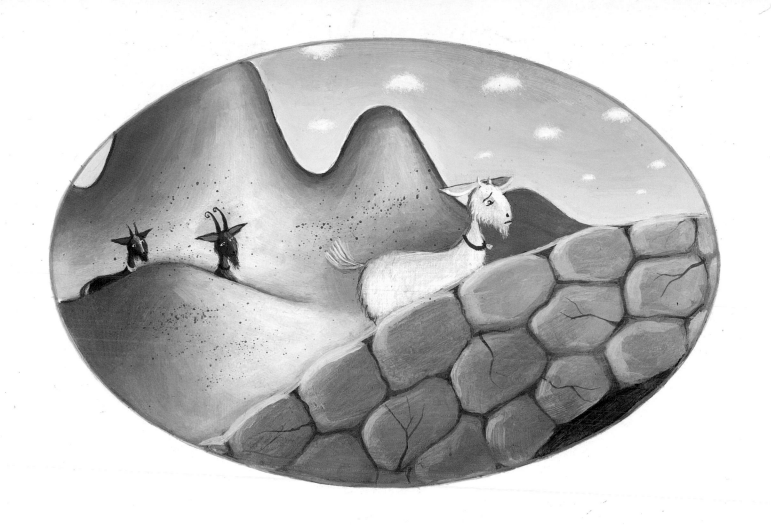

قالَ التَيسُ جروفْ الأول: "إِنّي جائِعٌ, وَ سَوفَ آكلُ هذا العُشبَ الشديدِ الخضرةِ". وَجرى قبلَ أنْ يَتمكّنَ الآخرانِ مِنْ إِيقافِهِ. جرى يُطقطقُ و يُطقطقْ عَبرَ الجِسرِ و عِندها...

"I'm hungry!" said the first Billy Goat Gruff. "And I'm going to eat that fresh green grass," and before the others could stop him, off he ran.
**Trip trap**, **trip trap** across the bridge he went when ...

سَمِعَ صوتاً يُزمجرُ: "مَنْ هذا الذي يُطقطقُ عَلى جِسري؟"
رَدَّ التَيس الأصغر بِصوتٍ مُنخفضٍ مُرتعشٍ: " أنا."

a voice roared: "Who's that **trip trapping** on **my** bridge?"
"It's only me," said the youngest Billy Goat Gruff, in a tiny, trembling voice.

زَمجرَ المارِدُ: "حسناً, أنا لَئيمٌ و جائِعٌ وَسوفَ آكُلُكَ!"
تَوَسَّلَ التَيسُ الأصغر: "أَرجوكَ لا تأكلنيْ, أنا صغيرٌ و نحيلٌ.
سيأتي أخي وَ هوَ أكبرُ منّي بِكثير."

"Well, I'm mean, and I'm hungry and I'm going to eat you up!" growled the Troll.
"Please, don't eat me. I'm only little and thin. My brother is coming and he's much much
bigger than me," pleaded the youngest Billy Goat Gruff.

وافقَ المارِدُ وَ قالَ: "حسناً. هذا صحيحْ. ما أنتَ ألا جلدٌ و عظم, وَ ليسَ بجسمِكَ لحمْ. سأنتظرُ أخاكَ الأكبر." وَهكذا عَبَرَ التيس الأول جروفْ اَلجِسر وَ بدأ في أكلِ العشبَ شديدِ الخضرة.

"Well yes, you *are* all skin and bones," agreed the Troll. "There's no meat on you.
I'll wait for your bigger brother."
So the first Billy Goat Gruff crossed over the bridge and started to eat the fresh green grass.

قالَ التَيسُ الثاني جروفْ: "إِذا كانَ أخي الصغير قدْ تَمكّنَ مِنْ عُبورِ الجسرِ, فَسَأتمكنُ أنا أيضاً!"
وَ بَدأ يُطقطقُ وَ يُطقطقْ عَبرَ الجِسرِ وَ عِندها...

The second Billy Goat Gruff said, "If my little brother can cross the bridge, then so can I!"
**Trip trap, trip trap** across the bridge he went when ...

سَمِعَ صوتاً يُزمجِرُ وَ يقول: " مَنْ هذا الذي يُطقطقُ على جِسري؟"
رَدَّ التَيس الأوسط جروفْ بِصوتٍ منخفضٍ خائِف: "أنا"

a voice roared: "Who's that **trip trapping** on **my** bridge?"
"It's only me," said the middle Billy Goat Gruff, in a small, scared voice.

زَمجرَ المارِدُ: "حسناً, أنا لئيمٌ وَ جائعٌ وَ سوفَ آكُلُكَ!"
تَوسّلَ التَيسُ الأوسطُ: "أرجوكَ لا تأكُلَني, أنا صغيرٌ وَ نحيل.
سيأتي أخي وَ هوَ أكبرُ مِنّي بِكثير."

"Well, I'm mean, and I'm hungry and I'm going to eat you up!" growled the Troll.
"Please don't eat me. I'm only little and thin. My other brother is coming and he's
much much bigger than me," pleaded the middle Billy Goat Gruff.

افقَ المارِدُ وَ قالَ: "حسناً. هذا صحيح. ما أنتَ ألا جِلدٌ و عظم, وَ ليسَ بِجسمِكَ لحمٌ كافي. سأنتظرُ أخاكَ الأكبر."
وَ هكذا عَبَرَ التيس الثاني جروفْ الجِسر وَ بَدأَ في أكلِ العشب شديدِ الخضرة.

"That's true, you *are* all skin and bones," agreed the Troll. "There's not enough meat on you. I'll wait for your bigger brother."
So the second Billy Goat Gruff crossed over the bridge and started to eat the fresh green grass.

وَ الآن أصبحَ التَيسانِ في المراعي شديدةِ الخضرةِ وَ بَقيَ تَيسٌ واحدٌ جائعٌ جداً.
فَكيفَ يُمكنُ للتَيسِ الثالثِ الأكبر جروفْ أنْ يَعبُرَ الجسرَ؟

Now there were two billy goats in the fresh green meadow and one very
hungry billy goat left behind.
How could the third and oldest Billy Goat Gruff cross over the bridge?

فَكَّرَ التَيسُ الثالثُ جروفْ: "حسناً. إِذا كانَ التَيسانِ الآخرانِ قدْ تمكَّنا مِن عُبور ذلكَ الجِسر فَسأتمكَّنُ أنا مِن ذلكَ.
وَ بدأً يُطقطقُ وَ يُطقطقْ عَبرَ الجِسر وَ عِندها...

"Well," thought the third Billy Goat Gruff, "if the others can cross that bridge then so can I!"
**Trip trap**, **trip trap** across the bridge he went when ...

سَمِعَ صوتاً يُزمجِرُ وَ يَقولُ: "مَنْ هذا الذي يُطقطقُ على جِسري؟"
هَدَرَ التيسُ الأكبر جروفْ: "أنا. إِنَني كَبيرٌ وَ قويٌ وَ لَستُ خائفاً مِنكَ!"
رغمَ أَنهُ كانَ خائفاً حقيقةً.

a voice roared: "Who's that **trip trapping** on **my** bridge?"
"It's me!" bellowed the oldest Billy Goat Gruff. "And I'm big, and I'm strong,
and I'm not scared of you!" - although he really was.

زَمجرَ المارِدُ قائلاً: "حسناً. إِنَني لَئيمٌ وَ جائِعٌ وَ سَوفَ آكُلُكَ!"

رَدَ التيسُ الأكبر جروفْ قائلاً: "هذا ما تَظنُهُ أنتَ. قَدْ تَكونُ لَئيماً وَ جائعاً وَ لكِنْ إِذا أرِدّتَ اِلتِهامي, فَها أنا ذا, تَعالَ اِليَ."

"Well, I'm mean, and I'm hungry and I'm going to eat you up!" growled the Troll.
"That's what you think!" said the oldest Billy Goat Gruff. "You may be mean,
and you may be hungry. But if you want to eat me, come and get me."

تَسَلَّقَ المارِدُ الجِسرَ وَ أَسرَعَ نَحوَ التَيسِ الثالثِ جروفْ.

The Troll climbed onto the bridge and rushed towards the third Billy Goat Gruff.

وَ لكنْ التَيس الثالث جروفْ كانَ مُستعداً لَهُ, فَخَفَضَ قرنيهِ, وَ ضَرَبَ الأرضَ بِحوافرِهِ يُطقطقُ وَ يُطقطقْ وَ هَجَمَ على المارِدِ.

But the third Billy Goat Gruff was ready for him. He lowered his horns, he stamped his hooves ... **trip trap, trip trap** ... and charged towards the Troll.

نَطَحَ التَيسُ الثالثُ جروفْ ذلكَ المارِدِ اللَئيمِ الجائعِ بِقرنَيهِ الكبيرَينِ الحادَّينِ.

The third Billy Goat Gruff butted that mean and hungry Troll with his big sharp horns.

طارَ المارِدُ في الهواءِ وَ هَبَطَ بِقوةٍ في الماءِ الباردِ فَتطايرَ الماءُ بِشدةٍ.

The Troll went flying through the air and landed
with a mighty splash, in the cold, cold water.

حَمَلَ النهرُ العميق جداً المارِدَ اللئيمَ الجائعَ بعيداً ألى البحرِ
وَ لمْ يَراهُ أحدٌ ألى الأبد.

The deep, deep river carried the mean and hungry Troll
out to sea and he was never seen again.

الآن لَمْ تَعُدْ التيوس الثلاثة جروفْ جائعة. وَ بِأمكانِها أن تَأكلَ العشب شديدِ الخضرةِ ما أرادَتْ. وَ أنْ تُطقطقَ وَ تُطقطقْ عَبرَ الجِسر متى شاءَتْ.

Now the three Billy Goats Gruff aren't hungry anymore.
They can eat as much fresh green grass as they want.
And they can **trip trap** across the bridge whenever they like.

*For Debbie, Sara, Katey, Jimbo, Rob & all the trolls!*
*H.B.*

*To Mum, Dad, Laura & David*
*R.J.*

First published in 2001 by Mantra Lingua
Global House, 303 Ballards Lane, London N12 8NP
www.mantralingua.com

Text copyright © 2001 Henriette Barkow
Illustration copyright © 2001 Richard Johnson
Dual language text copyright © Mantra Lingua
Audio copyright © 2008 Mantra Lingua

This sound enabled edition published 2014

Printed in UK